™

Let's Go, Irish!™

Aimee Aryal

Illustrated by Anuj Shrestha

MASCOT BOOKS®

www.mascotbooks.com

It was a beautiful fall day at
The University of Notre Dame.

The Leprechaun was on his way to
Notre Dame Stadium to watch
a football game.

He walked to the
Basilica of the Sacred Heart.
The bells began to chime.

A priest walked past and said,
"Let's go, Irish!"

The Leprechaun passed the
Main Building and stopped to
admire the Gold Dome.

A group of students standing nearby
said, "Let's go, Irish!"

The Leprechaun went by
Saint Mary's Lake. He stopped
at the Grotto of Our Lady of Lourdes.

A couple walking by said,
"Let's go, Irish!"

The Leprechaun walked to
Hesburgh Library. He stopped
and looked at the mural.

He went inside to return a book.
The librarian whispered,
"Let's go, Irish!"

It was almost time for the football game.
As the Leprechaun walked to the
stadium, he passed by some alumni.

The alumni remembered the Leprechaun
from their days at Notre Dame.
They said, "Let's go, Irish!"

Finally, the Leprechaun arrived at
Notre Dame Stadium -
"The House that Rockne Built."

As he ran onto the football field,
the Leprechaun cheered,
"Let's go, Irish!"

The Leprechaun watched the game
from the sidelines and
cheered for the team.

The Fighting Irish scored six points!
The quarterback shouted,
"Touchdown, Leprechaun!"

At halftime,
The Band of the Fighting Irish
performed on the field.

The Leprechaun and
the crowd listened to
"The Notre Dame Victory March."

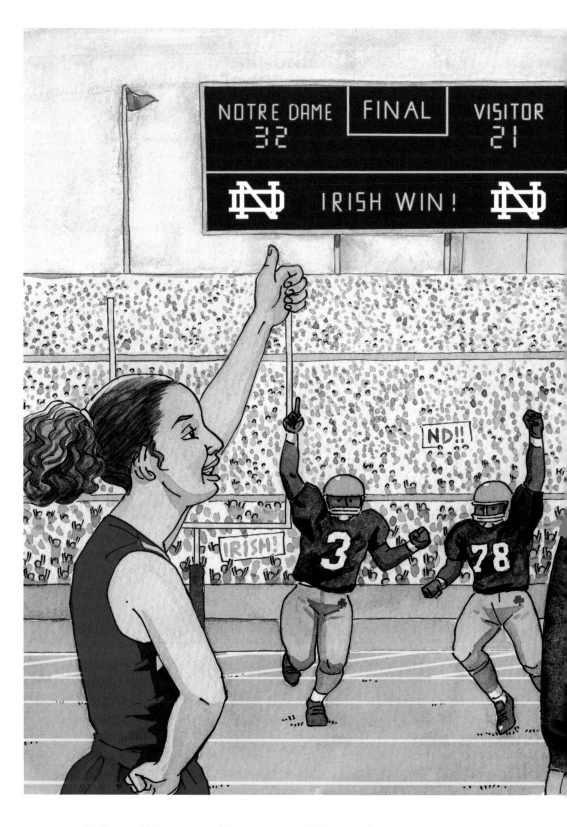

The Notre Dame Fighting Irish
won the football game!

The Leprechaun gave the coach
a high-five. The coach said,
"Great game, Leprechaun!"

After the football game, the Leprechaun
was tired. It had been a long day
at the University of Notre Dame.

He walked home and climbed into bed.

Goodnight, Leprechaun.

For Anna and Maya, and all of
the Leprechaun's little fans. ~ AA

This book is dedicated with love
to my grandmother, Shanti Devi Bhandari. ~ AS

For more information about our products, please visit us online at www.mascotbooks.com.

For more information, please contact Mascot Books,
P.O. Box 220157, Chantilly, VA 20153-0157

ISBN: 0-9743442-5-7

Printed in the United States.

www.mascotbooks.com